TIMES SQUARE

To Katie,

Here's to all the words
and all the wonders
you'll discover in this
amazing city.

Very Best,

Rick Wall

BY RICH WALLS

Standby, Chicago
One Page Love Story
Times Square

TIMES SQUARE

a novella

Rich Walls

CUNNING BOOKS
NEW JERSEY

First Edition.

ISBN 978-0-9913762-3-0
Also available in E-Book Formats

Cover Design by Rebecca N. Johnson
Design for Publication by 52 Novels

www.richwalls.net

To my New York.
To your New York.

1

"THIS ISN'T IT," she thinks, tracing sleet on the windowpane while her husband speaks, thankful to be inside rather than out, when a knock sounds from the door.

"Hold on," she says, tossing her phone on the bed so she can don a sweater.

Through the peephole stands a night manager fixing the pin on his lapel.

She opens the door.

The manager lifts his head, a wry smile caught beneath clear frame glasses. His pin, she notices, is in the shape of a snowflake.

"Good evening," she says.

"Yes, it is a good evening," he laughs. "A very good evening indeed."

"Can I help you?" she asks.

"No, no. It is I who can help you," he responds, swinging his right arm forward. "A letter, hand delivered, at special request."

She accepts the envelope. It is ice blue and thick. Written on front, in a swirling silver script, is her name.

"Who sent this?" she asks.

"I am only a messenger. Perhaps the answer is inside."

"I understand, thank you," she says, stepping backwards.

"You're very welcome," he replies in place.

"I'm sorry, should I tip?"

"No, that is not necessary," he waves.

"Is there anything else then?" she asks, imagining this amused manager standing guard outside her door until morning.

Instead, a remarkably sincere expression washes over his face.

"Only that I'll be wishing you a very good night, Mrs. Hart. Sometimes that is all we can wish for—a very good night."

The manager tips his head in courtesy and strides down the hallway, his suit jacket flapping wide. She watches until he rounds the corner before she closes the door.

"Sorry," she says, returning to her phone.

"What did I miss?"

"Just a porter. Delivering the bill, I think. What did you say you were doing?"

"Flipping through our wedding album."

"That's right," she answers as she turns the envelope in her hand. "You said you picked a favorite?"

"The one of us dancing."

"Which one?" she asks. On the back of the blue envelope is a white wax seal. She traces its raised edges with her fingertip. Pressed within is a snowflake.

"The wide shot. In the background, total darkness, completely black. In the foreground, barely off-center, you and I. I'm a silhouette, but you, along with your dress—it's the perfect white. Your chin on my shoulder..."

She tears the envelope.

"...and Colby Wilson singing..."

Inside is a single folded card embossed with a matching snowflake.

"...and you," he speaks but she does not hear. "Do you remember what you said?"

She unfolds the card, feels her breath catch within her chest.

"Angie?"

"Yes?" she asks.

"Do you remember what you said?"

"What did I say?" she responds, hands shaking.

"'Forever.' You said, 'This. Forever.'"

How would he have known?

"I love you, Angie."

Angie returns to the sleet-pocked window. Across, the Marquis hovers like a fifty-story switchboard, squares of yellow blinking through the storm. Below, bursts of rainbow light bombard 46th Street in silence, like peering into the world's largest living room late at night and discovering the T.V. left on.

This isn't it, she reminds herself. There is nothing out there for her. Nothing old and nothing new. Certainly nothing in the wet cold. She left it behind long ago.

But it does seem familiar, she thinks, fingering the charm around her neck.

As if it hasn't been that long at all.

As if she could close her eyes and see through each of these buildings. Place every landmark and place herself anywhere in this city.

At any time.

With, it seems, anyone.

"What was that?" she asks her husband.

"I love you, Angie."

Far too familiar.

"I love you, too."

Do you remember falling in love?

St. Dymphna's. 9 P.M.

2

HE WAS LATE.

Angie swished her cider and eavesdropped on the three square tables of international misfits beside her. They were young and boisterous and their accents each sung with promises of places she might rather be. She nicknamed them 'The U.N.,' which they very well could have been, junior delegates or interns, and listened as she waited.

"No! The bear would eat the shark!" shouted the German in the group.

"But it would be in water," replied a South African. "In the water, the shark would eat the bear! We have sharks. I am telling you. The shark would win."

"You have wussy bears then. German bears would eat the shark."

"Pretty, not-quite-blonde girl, sitting by herself," spoke a Belgian, turning towards Angie who had hid herself poorly, "who would win, a bear or a shark?"

"They both would lose by fighting," Angie answered. "The winner would be the fish that got away."

"Ahhh, she is pretty and intelligent," replied the Belgian.

The German booed. "A German bear would eat the shark and then chase the fish for fun."

"Your German bear would not last two seconds!"

"And your unadaptable shark could not survive on a mountain."

"This is stupid," interjected one of two Spanish men. "Why don't we agree the shark would lose on land and the bear would lose in water?"

"Do not underestimate the German bear!"

"I have another question for the pretty American girl," spoke the Belgian. "Do you know Marilyn Monroe?"

"Yes," Angie answered.

"Does my girlfriend not look just like Marilyn Monroe?" He gestured towards the Japanese girl sitting beside him.

Angie laughed. Clearly the girlfriend looked nothing like Marilyn Monroe, but she was gorgeous. Her hair especially—black oil paint swathed across a pristine canvas.

"Prettier," Angie said. "Prettier than Marilyn Monroe."

The table ooh'ed and aah'ed before the Belgian erupted, loud enough for the entire barroom to hear, "My girlfriend is more pretty than Marilyn Monroe!"

"Answer me this," interjected Charles, appearing like a gleeful ghost. "Does my date not look like Ingrid Bergman?"

As the Belgian considered, Angie wondered how Charles had entered without her seeing.

"Elle est parfaite," the Belgian said at last. "Magnifique. More beautiful than any actress on the silver screen."

"Did you hear that?" Charles turned to Angie. "You are more beautiful than any actress ever to grace the screen."

"And you're late," Angie replied.

"I am late, and I am sorry. But I do have an excuse," he declared, taking a seat across the small square table. "I made you a gift."

"You made me a gift?" she asked.

"Yes."

"What is it?"

"Soon, you will see."

"When?"

"When the time is right."

And then he winked.

Her grandfather's wink. Thief from the start. Her grandmother once called it his maddening trait, that her husband could be dead wrong, caught in the proverbial coat roam, bloody dagger in hand, but then he would wink. Impervious, he would shutter his eye and brandish a grin, as if to say, "It's all come to plan, hasn't it?"

So here was Charles, twenty minutes late, winking.

All to plan.

"Were you waiting long?" he asked, failing to smother his grin.

"No, not long," she answered.

"Well, I am sorry."

"It's fine," she accepted, despite adding a delayed, "Thank you," to dig the wound.

Only encouraged, Charles asked if she had been to this bar before.

"No," she answered.

"The first time I ever came to Dymphna's, a bandmate told me, 'You will never come here and not make a friend.' Four years later, it's still true. Just like you, it appears," he nodded towards Angie's U.N.

"Hello Ingrid Bergman!" yelled the Belgian, catching their glance.

"Hello," Angie answered with a brusque wave. They seemed sweet, perfect maybe for another night, but new friends had not been her reason for coming.

"Dates are boring," the Belgian shouted back. "Move closer. You drink with us."

She turned to Charles for support.

To her horror, he looked ecstatic.

"What do you think?" he asked, a wink no doubt coiling. "Should we make some friends?"

Angie dug a nail into her palm, recalled how he had originally two-stepped out of Strand, returning only to apologize a second time that he would have stayed for a longer book talk were he not already late for *breakfast* in Meatpacking even though it had been near ten P.M.

It was too late to back out now, but she had known it then: he was a child like the rest.

"Come on," he added. "It'll be fun."

She cringed at the word. A religion in this city. The obsession to find it. The ever-achievable, always just out of reach brass ring. For those who lack the eloquence or awareness to state what they're actually looking for. 'I like having *fun*.'

She sighed audibly. Glanced about the yellow room with its bare walls and dancing shadows. Peered through her flickering cider. Those colors. She would dream in them if she could choose. And then towards Charles with his shaggy hair and saucer eyes. A puppy, really. Spin him around and find a tail snapping back and forth. So eager to please and be pleased.

He balled his hands as if to beg. She offered him no sympathy. He fake bit his knuckles. She returned a stone face until she noticed his fingertips were stained blue and she laughed.

Why wouldn't they be?

It felt like a crime that no date could ever be just a date. Some universal grievance held against her. But also, she realized, what did that make her—the girl who would say no to a night like this: a cozy barroom, an eager boy, the great nations of the world beside.

Believe, she told herself. Even if you don't.

Have a little *fun*.

"Okay," she answered at last, sending Charles into orbit. "But first I need to use the ladies' room."

"Another cider, was it?"

Give him that—Charles, always observant.

"Yes, please."

Angie stood as he slid their wooden table the ten short inches alongside The U.N. She passed the twelve-stool bar lit like a memory beneath Christmas lights. In back, through a windowed door, a couple braved a miniature courtyard, huddling over a single candle as if it held winter's last warmth. She spun into the bathroom on the right.

The inside was dark. She patted for a switch. When she found it, a pale light revealed a bare black box with only a sink and a toilet.

Bare except for the walls, that is—subway tiles with a blackboard finish, graffiti chalked on every inch. She read the scrawls as she nested the seat: *yr bf keeps staring at me; AD/CB; The Cubes are overrated, your overrated, your grammar is overrated.*

Turning to unbutton, she caught sight of a large blue arrow pointing up from above the mirrorless sink.

Directly overhead was a snowflake. Its center—the light fixture itself. A small dull circle flat against the ceiling. But its outer arms stretched in exceedingly elaborate patterns of chalk. Fractals upon fractals, sparkling it seemed, practically gleaming, which itself seemed impossible—how could anything gleam within the lightless vacuum of an East Village bathroom? Yet, this snowflake gleamed.

Her eyes fell to the bottom of the image. There, she saw inscribed, in perfect cursive, chalk fresh as snow, *"Angie's Snowflake."*

Angie burst from the bathroom, nearly toppling a bubble-jacketed girl standing in wait.

"Sorry!" she shouted backwards as she sprinted past the bar.

Charles, in mid-conversation with the German, turned and spoke before she ever said a word.

"Hello, Snowflake. I'm sorry I was late."

3

THEY ALL LOOK like children.

Many are—the would-be pop stars exiting McDonald's, the Penny skateboarders crackling down St. Marks like rolling fire—but even those old enough, those who are the same age she was then, it seems too soon.

Angie passes a girl sitting cross-legged on the frozen wet sidewalk, her head bowed and bouncing like she's counting down a game of Hide 'n Seek. Angie pauses close enough to hear: it is the refrain from *Friends* she chants, fifteen years too late.

How did anyone think this was a good idea? Nothing but children without supervision. Like walking into a real life Neverland. Second star on the right, straight on 'til morning.

Of course, she remembers, that was the appeal, too. A chance to grow up. Out every night, practicing stares of raccoon-eyed scorn at any boy who appeared to care.

Total freedom. The opportunity to make mistakes. To learn being a witch does bring short term benefits, and later, long term consequences.

Which hardly makes this Neverland at all, she realizes. The goal was never to stay young. It was to have a playground without teachers. A place to learn life's lessons without being taught.

And she succeeded. Far be it to tell her the life lessons would be bittersweet.

St. Dymphna's appears, faded yellow like a favorite tee rediscovered at the bottom of a drawer. She wishes she could do this in private, say goodbye to this place alone, but she knows another favorite waits within.

She pictures Charles seated inside, like a boy at his birthday table, hands folded while his knees piston underneath, and steels herself as she opens the door.

Their corner is empty.

Of him, at least. Same as the rest of the room after two glances.

No surprise, probably to plan, he is late.

Angie approaches the bar and orders her cider anyhow, this day demanding a drink, before choosing a table between the window and a young couple dressed up like it's Homecoming. She wants to have eyes on Charles from every direction.

She checks her phone. Thankfully, there are no messages from Geoffrey. They will sit down tomorrow, she decides. She will open a bottle of wine and she will say what needs saying, sticking to the truth: It was a lark. Not even meant to be real. Totally unexpected and, well—swallowing her guilt—at least Geoffrey's always been good with the truth. She only hopes he's found a better way to spend his night than flipping through their wedding album.

"Excuse me, ma'am," asks the boy beside her. "Would you mind taking our picture?"

"Sure," Angie answers, excusing the *ma'am* and reaching for his phone. "Where you from?"

"Oklahoma. I moved here in January. She'll be coming after she graduates in May."

"I guess I shouldn't tell you I'm U.T. then," Angie replies.

"Oh, no!" the girl cries, pure Okie.

"Don't worry," Angie appeases. "I'm really good at pictures. Follow me, ready? Hook 'em Horns on three."

Their faces squeeze sour.

"Fine," she corrects. "New York, on three. One. Two."

"New York!"

Flash and Angie captures a picture that is frankly adorable even to her. His zits and team captain's chin still developing. Her cheeks, she thinks, never left the bassinette.

"Aw, thank you!" the girl shouts. "It came out perfect."

"You're welcome," Angie replies, checking the door for Charles.

"Do you have any advice?" the girl asks.

Angie spins back and pauses at the sweetness of the question.

The girl, wearing his blazer, belongs in *Seventeen.* So cheery even her back molars glow nice-to-meet-you. So proper she's squared her shoulders to Angie and pinned her hands to her left hip like it's portrait day, pompoms hidden at her feet.

Right behind, the boy, still in his tie, has his arms wrapped about her. Proud boyfriend, proud protector, proud host in his big new city.

Stay perfect, she wants to answer, noticing the way they sit side by side, taking up two tables. You may think you want this, and maybe you do, but please, hold on to whatever you are now. As long as you can. This place will take it away before you knew you had something to lose.

But of course that's nothing they could understand. Not yet anyway. So she encourages them to, "Enjoy it," adding, "It goes quick," another advice they won't actually understand, but typical enough to humble them for the length of a sip, energize them with visions of that great dangling lollipop of life lying ahead.

"We will!" the girl bursts, so genuinely Angie wonders if she had accidentally waxed profound.

She is glad when the boy raises his glass, offering a celebratory punctuation. "To New York!" he says.

"Yes," Angie tips her cider. "To New York."

The girl, overwhelmed, nuzzles her head into her boyfriend's chest—nowhere else in the world she would rather be. In return, he squeezes her tight as he can and kisses her brushed-to-silk chocolatey crown.

Angie turns away.

Across the room, three friends sit at what was once her table. No, never officially, but the one she always gravitated to with its bench seating and the view of the street with its parading passerby. The odd way the wall on her back always felt comforting, drawing her in to whomever she sat with.

So many nights parked right there. Beginning with Charles. Those spinning nights with Charles. Then the promise to never return without him. *Anyone but dates.* That was their agreement. Later, a break of that promise, under fair circumstances, but not without guilt.

Geoffrey, she recalls, came after. It was an accident. She had cornered herself admitting to being free one same night after cancelling on him for the next. "Dymphna's," she had said, without even thinking.

Soon he became a habit, always returning to Dymphna's because he believed it to be her favorite. In retrospect, it was a miracle they never ran into Charles, although he never reserved himself to one bar either. If, in the end, Angie had one Dymphna's, Charles may have had seven or eight.

But, in one regard, it was true. After a time she did refer to this place as *her* Dymphna's. Never *ours* as Geoffrey liked to say—that phrase always irking Angie, the assumed ownership of something which was someone else's before. But she never corrected him either. Geoffrey was happy. Let him be so. Maybe most shocking of all, with a life and city she had finally remolded to her liking, she had been happy, too.

She checks her phone. 9:26. Late now, even for Charles.

She wonders, what must be the point? He could have texted, he could have called. Doesn't he know she would have answered?

But then, also, why now? Five years since they last spoke, six since they dated. Don't feelings disappear after so long?

Or maybe they don't. Making her the bigger fool for coming. For giving him hope.

Because that's all this will be, all it can be, she determines. A quick, Hi-Charles-it's-good-to-see-you-but-really-I-can't-I'm-married-I'm-sorry-but-I-hope-you're-doing-well.

Except for the part that is steadily unnerving her, her eyeliner addicted alter ego from a decade ago rising up within—that an ounce of her hopes he'll plead for her again.

Because, well—saying this to no one else—wouldn't that be nice.

And also, because, what then...

Angie digs her ring into her thumb. Clears her wandering mind.

This bar. These barely grown-up children. Let them serve as reminder:

She is thirty-five.

She did grow up.

She sets her glass and rises for the bathroom. If the walls are blank, she will call Charles, tell him she never came. Their Dymphna's died long ago.

She passes the bar still lit like perpetual Christmas. She remembers the time Charles accidentally spilled beer on a stranger and immediately poured the rest on himself to prevent a fight. The stranger thought it was terrific. Angie called him a child and left.

Just like she will be in ten seconds.

She opens the door.

Fishes for the light. Flips it.

A row of stick figures greet her. With great big smiley faces and loopy hair drawn using every color from the box. They hold red and green squares high above their heads. On the wall, wiped clean above:

You always loved people watching...

4

"I KNOW I'VE asked you this before, but are you sure?"

Hector squinted towards the piano where Teddy stood with arms wrapped around two men, one whose snowy hair matched his pinstripes, the other an Adonis flaunting a skintight t-shirt, the three together teetering on the verge of collapse as they serenaded the wooden beams directly above them.

"I'm sure," Angie answered.

"Joking, you know," Hector added.

"I know."

"Course every joke has a grain of truth."

Angie shot Hector an accusatory look to which he raised his hands and shoe brush eyebrows up, *don't shoot.*

"He would have made his move years ago," Angie sighed with an image of Teddy in her mind. "He's stuck with me."

"And vice versa."

"Yes, and vice versa," she agreed, still picturing Teddy bundled across her chest the way so many nights ended, same as she expected this one would: her fingering his curls while his hands roamed quietly.

No, Teddy wasn't going anywhere.

"You're good to him, Angie. Good *for* him."

"Am I?"

"Sure you are. Mature for your age."

"You think?"

"I do."

"What about him?" she asked, nodding towards her man, the six-foot-three stick of a boy currently unhinged by the sad comedy of an older woman's life.

"He'll get there. We all do."

"And when did you?"

"In many different stages," Hector answered, pausing in disgust. "Please do not insist that was a pun."

"I'd never," Angie laughed.

Hector rolled his eyes and turned his head, catching a lyric as it floated past. He sang to Angie, dark eyes and blown cheeks come alive, "*Is it true you were mine, 'til I paid you mind? If so, here, I'll go.*"

The song drifted ahead as Hector reached for his wine. Such was his way. Two lines and release. Ask for more and he would smile coyly, "I'm retired."

"How long have you two been together?" he asked Angie.

"Five-and-a-half years."

"And you're how old?"

"Twenty-four."

Hector's face sagged in revulsion. "Swore you were twenty-six."

"Nope, twenty-four," Angie repeated proudly.

"You know when I was twenty-four I had legs like a Roman statue."

"And you had to pry Gwen Goshen off of you."

"Did I tell you that story?"

"Mmm-hmm," Angie nodded.

"A sign we're getting to know each other too well. I'd hate for you to think I'd run out of stories."

"And I'd hate for you to stop sharing them."

"Words to make an actor blush. But back to you. You are twenty-four, you have been dating for five years. Angie Seaglass, smoothed by the sea, I ask you, is that thin-limbed student of Stephen Sondheim and J. Crew the man you intend to spend the grand sweeping epic of your life with?"

Not even a question, she thought, the answer so positively yes. She could detail the entire arc:

The night an engineering student twice her height from New York waltzed her to her dorm all the way from Sixth Street. Afterwards, while brushing her teeth, re-alization—her inner voice practically squealing from across the mirror, 'Everything's changed, Angie. With that boy, everything's changed.'

Destiny fulfilling itself their last night in Austin. With sweet Daniel Johnston echoing from her laptop beside them, Teddy described how she had become his memory of Texas. How excited he was that she would become his memory of New York.

Skepticism tossed aside these two years when that is exactly what came to pass. The dream was always to make it to New York. The adventure would reveal itself then. How unexpected the city would become so synonymous with a boy.

Yes, she thought to herself. Unequivocally yes. Her mind had been made up for the day Teddy would finally ask.

But why jinx it?

So she answered Hector, with a bite of her lip, "I guess we'll see."

"Why do I try?" he groaned. "I give you the nitty-gritty on what it's like to be a classically trained dancing tea cup on Broadway and you give me 'I guess we'll see.'"

"You know you're my favorite."

"Favorite. We just toss around words, don't we?" he quipped as Teddy tripped into view, his hand landing on Angie's lap.

"I'mgonnahaveonemore," he blurted.

"You sure?" Angie asked.

"Inee—," he stuttered, "Ineedonemore."

"Need?"

Teddy's eyes fell as he sought her hand, grasping in a strange and unusually loving way. Not a pleading beg, but slowly squeezing, observing the act of their hands together, then her face in front of his, and back and forth, as if he had found something he feared might disappear, and Angie thought to ask whether he was okay when at last he marbled, "Razzledazzle," and spun around for the piano, bar forgotten.

"Like I said," Hector chimed, rubbing his thick goatee. "Good *for* him."

Angie did not respond. She watched Teddy perform once more to the ceiling. Wondered who he was singing to really, what chord this place struck inside. He never said. Was it as simple as all those shows he had seen with his mother growing up? Was it that no one else but Angie knew this existed for him? Smiling, always happy

Teddy. Friend to everybody, but who scarcely believed he had a friend. So unwilling to let anybody in.

It seemed such a lonely, self-created place.

Still, she was glad it existed. Not his struggle, if he had one, but the feeling there was some string of beauty seen only to him. She might never see it, but she was sure he did. Maybe it floated here beneath the wooden beams and he saw it when he closed his eyes. Touched it, she knew, when he touched her skin.

That was the Teddy no one else knew. The real Teddy. The Teddy who loved musicals and felt and reached for beauty outside of common sight, outside the pre-drawn world in which he lived.

If only he had kept reaching.

That night he called Angie from their Hell's Kitchen bedroom out on to the couch where he sat in the dark with his head bobbing. He took her hand, tighter than he had at Marie's, and, fighting a wave of hiccups, found the courage to tell Angie that his father had found him a job in Dubai, that it was a really good opportunity, he would soon be leaving for at least two years, and even though he loved her more than anyone else on Earth, maybe it just might not be any more than that.

5

WALKER.

Washington.

Waverly—

"Can I help you find something?" asks a monotone voice.

The dangling lanyard beside Angie's squatting head introduces, "*Simon.*" Behind, a once navy t-shirt deadpans, "*cool font,*" in Helvetica. Much higher is a spectacled cousin of Paul Bunyan she does not recognize.

"I think I've nearly—," Weston, Wicket, *Wilcox*. "Got it," she answers, removing the thick volume.

So it does exist.

The Autobiography of Charles Wilcox: To Be Written Primarily After His Death (Being So Busy With Living).

"Oh," Simon grunts. "*That* book."

"You know it?" Angie asks.

"Yes," he answers dryly. "It's too steady to drop and too stupid to support," he blinks, catching himself. "No offense."

Angie laughs as she spins the bulk in her hand. 742 pages. Exactly as Charles envisioned.

"Do you know him?" Simon asks.

"I do."

"I feel like most people do. I think he might be the most famous non-famous person I know."

"That describes him perfectly, actually," she responds, flipping back to the front. "Does he sell a lot of these?"

"At least seven or eight a month."

A mellow pride whirls within Angie, imagining how pleased Charles must be with himself. Not for the money, there couldn't be much, but for all its pocket affirmations.

That he brought a whimsy to door-stopping life.

That he can answer, "Me too," to anyone who gloats, "I'm in Strand," without humility at a party.

That, and this most of all, the joke exists entirely in tribute to his labyrinth of friends. Why else would seven people a month, three years later, enter the city's most famous bookstore and exit $24.95 lighter with a hardbound brick whose sole paragraph runs

Prologue

My mother taught me the three keys to life: Always finish what you start, believe in everyone you meet, and never, no matter what,

straight off a cliff, 741 numbered-but-empty pages following.

" 'Cause the joke is," she remembers him trying to explain, and she had to stop him, "I got it."

She rubs his sailor's portrait on the cover. Brave explorer in a red knit beanie. Bloodline to Hemingway or Cousteau. Ask him: maybe both.

"What you can't see," she feels the need to share with Simon, a morsel privy only to her, "is the financial district cropped out over here," pointing right of the picture. "It's the Staten Island Ferry. We finished a box of Franzia on the top deck."

"Ah," Simon's eyes glow sarcastically. "The mystery unravels."

Angie opens the book again, searching for the clue she must have missed. It is not on the title page or the dedication page (A vaguely inclusive, *"To you."*). Or page one. She flips through the individually numbered pages. All blank. The back cover, too. Empty.

She checks the shelf for other copies. None are there. Not even space for one beside it.

"This isn't—" she says aloud.

"It's not?" Simon asks.

"No, it is. It's just, I'm supposed to find—" and she wonders, what *is* she supposed to find? "My favorite book?"

"Well, what's your favorite book?"

"That's the thing," she answers. "I don't have one."

The comedy of her Strand infatuation come to a head: for most her life, she barely read.

It had been The Dark Years waning. A decision she wanted to find someone again. Tired of aimless nights, she hoped to meet a boy she could share her days with.

The image came to her of a boy who reads. She did not know the rest—did not know if he would wear vests and discuss philosophy, still play sports, or even write for himself—she did not care. If he had a book in his hand, that made sense.

She dove in, visiting Strand on sunless Sunday afternoons in November, aiming for the anti-football crowd and discovering the base definition of crowd instead, the bookstore so packed with shoppers romantic opportunities began and ended with, "Excuse me."

A change in tactic and she discovered the unique joy of weeknights at Strand. When nine P.M. browsing felt like a scene from *Nighthawks*. Books replacing coffee as strangers stilled themselves in contemplation, the floorboards creaking with each shifting step. Beneath a halo of fluorescence, the feeling they had each found shelter from a dark and vacant city, arrived in light with similar purpose. So what if that purpose might have little to do with reading.

She purchased books out of guilt, piled them into columns in her bedroom. She even read some, struggling to find a spark. Fiction she found too fictional. Poetry, like painting, pretty, but who's to say? Self-help, a road to self-loathing. Business the anti-escape. And on, until one night, Penelope, her lanyarded Sherpa through much of three months, handed her the memoir of Katherine Bennington, a socialite-turned-philanthropist who spent a year living within New York's tenements.

The pilot light struck. At twenty-seven-years old, Angie Seaglass discovered her first reading passion: biographies.

Or, "People watching in book form," she joked, once too often perhaps.

Funny the way others caught on. The boy she ultimately met at Strand but did not marry, Charles—whom, in retrospect, Angie never saw purchase a book despite being on a first name basis with the entire staff—burst his autobiography pitch on her as a pick-up line. And poor Geoffrey, with all his gift cards over the years. He had seen her tote bag and assumed he had found her heart.

"Well, what about your least favorite book?" a visibly lost Simon now suggests. "Like, 'Hey, I found Charles Wilcox's autobiography. Really makes me want to go read so-and-so-else!'"

Angie's non-reaction defeats him.

"Okay," he says, "no more Charles Wilcox bashing."

"No, that's fine," she assures him, suddenly feeling defeated herself.

What, she wonders, is she chasing? Or why? The game as a straight line had been alluring, memory lane keeping her awake. But now the path's been lost, she feels the weight of the hour, ten o'clock, pressing against an already too long week, and is exhausted again.

She needs to straighten the line, she decides.

She needs to kill the ghosts.

"You know what," she says, raising Charles's book. "This is it. This is what I was looking for. Thank you, Simon."

"You're welcome?" he answers, dumfounded and, Angie expects, further convinced each of Charles's friends are completely nuts.

"Is there anything else?" he asks politely.

"No," she answers. "We nailed it."

"Cool," Simon shrugs, stepping backwards with a half wave. "Try not to finish that all in one night."

Angie reaches for her phone. Scrolls to Charles.

"*Hi,*" she texts, standing in place for his response. She senses he is close, can imagine the five years since they spoke as nothing at all. In minutes they will pick up a string where they left it. The only difference: she is now married while he has been waiting.

Her phone buzzes. On cue.

"*20 min?*"

About as long as it takes to walk.

"*Ok*," she replies in stride. As she rounds the aisle, she catches the glance of a man standing at the front of the store. Beneath clear frame glasses, a wry smile spreads.

It cannot be.

Why wouldn't it be?

The man nods above him. Suspended from the ceiling is a single glittering snowflake. Angie had been so focused on Charles's autobiography, she never bothered to look up.

With his eyes he traces a line down from the snowflake to a table of books where he taps the top of a pile.

"Keep going," he mouths. From across the store she cannot hear him, but she is certain those are his words.

Before she can ask, "Where?" he backs through the exit.

Angie sprints. On her third step, her hip catches a table of dangling paperbacks. Her mind splits as she halts to pick the fallen titles from the floor while visualizing her less clumsy self outside.

Racing again, she is nearly through the door when an arm bars her way.

"Excuse me, miss!" shouts the guard.

He points towards the bulk that is Charles's autobiography in her right hand. She dumps the book along with her purse and begs, "I'll be right back," as she races onto the sidewalk where the man with the clear glasses and knowing smile is nowhere in sight up or down Broadway or along 12th Street.

Flushed and panting, Angie re-enters Strand. Two dozen curious eyes follow her. To the guard she apologizes profusely—"I thought I saw a friend"—and promises to pay for Charles's book which she now retrieves along with her purse from the floor.

Backing slowly, she spins around. Ahead and just above her, the glittering snowflake twists from its dangling string.

Where it points to beneath is a table of coffee books, each themed around New York City: the skyline, the streets, landmarks, the people, and the parks.

Yellow cutouts highlight one-word staff reactions on each. *"Yum!"* for restaurants. *"Culture!"* for a book on museums.

At the very top, adorned by a glittered snowflake in place of a yellow superlative: *The High Line*.

Angie opens to the silver bookmark within. Beside a gorgeous photograph of her favorite white frame:

Don't forget to take a moment for yourself.

6

IF ONLY SHE could keep the view.

From this roof. Of this skyline.

High above all. Two billion lights shining.

If only she could pocket this somehow, open it up again from her own non-roof-accessible apartment.

Then she could keep it.

But the view came with the boy. It seemed a shame to let him down so soon.

"...which is how I ended up here," he said, finishing a decade-long story that had begun in Ann Arbor and weaved through several cities she had paid only partial attention to while considering ways to break the news gently.

"Do you miss Michigan?" she asked, tossing another softball to delay the event, offer her time to count the traits of his she might miss. Last lifelines before leaving him to drift.

He was punctual. Add that to the list: dependability. She wondered how she had ever put up with anything else. But Geoffrey showed up. That was nice.

He was a gentleman. In every sense of the word. The obvious things—the opening doors, the standing to greet her—but also the little stuff. Never a phone at the table. Eye contact which conveyed listening. In every instance, her comfort above all else.

An odd one: he liked sports. She had rarely dated sports fans, but that first date, after he fessed to missing Michigan's kickoff, she urged him to a bar and found Texas on next to his. The strange magnetism of college football. Long after her every tie to Austin had been severed, within minutes of seeing burnt orange on green grass...Dammit, it was *Go Horns, Go!* all over again.

Surprising how normal that felt. How red-blooded American. Beers and wings and absolute outcomes. Funny how much she enjoyed it.

"What about you?" he asked.

"Sorry?"

"Do you think you'll be here a long time?"

"I hope so. It's the only place I've ever wanted to be," she answered, suppressing a growing disillusionment, a question of how far that had gotten her, if she was better for it.

"That's neat," he said softly.

"That I like New York?"

"That you made it to the place you always wanted to be."

"Well you're here," she countered, not wanting credit for something so small.

"I don't think it ever occurred to me growing up this was possible. This," he raised his hands in tribute to the city, "this is a gift."

A familiar cynicism flashed and faded from her mind. The desire to call B.S. overwhelmed by a pang of regret—some bit of envy if she never painted the city in so warm a light, as anything other than an inevitability.

Beside her, the recipient of that gift, Geoffrey, sat casually with his fists-for-calves soccer legs propped up in his Adirondack chair, looking like a vacationer or a tourist, so at ease. So very pleased to be here.

"What—" he began and she cut him off.

"My turn," she said, not knowing if it were true.

"Okay," he laughed.

"The billionaire roommate. Real or not real?"

"Did we talk about A.J.?" he sifted through the fog of their Dymphna's night. "Definitely not a billionaire. Yet."

"How come I've never seen him? I looked in his room. There's nothing in there but a desk, a bed, and a poster of Michael Jordan."

"He lives in London with his family."

"And he keeps a place here?"

"For another five months anyway. We're moving out in February."

Angie winced. The loss of what was never hers. Moved on.

"Why an accountant?" she asked, the question more for her than for him. A test of how prepared she was to give up a life she had been missing—drinking from Tupperware in kitchens with chefs, celebrating post-shows upstairs at Spotted Pig with bands—for another more tame.

"Because I like numbers. I like the puzzle of it. It's useful. I'm good at it."

She pictured him in front of a monitor, making sense of a screen full of figures, and found she admired his dominion over something that would put her to sleep.

"Why are you so nice?" she continued, a dumb question, but on the pulse of a momentum she could feel building.

"Because I like it when others are."

Fair. Sweet.

"Why haven't you tried to kiss me yet?"

The question spilled from her. To the point she nearly covered her mouth, stopping only when she felt the relief of its release. She had not realized how badly she had wanted to ask him until she did.

"Ah," he laughed. "So you noticed."

"Yes, I noticed. It's been how many dates, six, seven? Most guys would have by now."

He stretched out his arms, his fingertips tapping tops of buildings in her vision like piano keys.

"I don't know if this is real, or me being superstitious," he said, "but it's never worked out when I kissed a girl too soon. The ones that did, the ones that mattered, they took time." He shifted in his chair, facing her. "I like you, Angie. I want you to matter."

A breeze blew past. She imagined it bouncing from one roof to the next and wished she could ride along with it, straight on down the avenue. Jump off somewhere near Battery Park.

I want you to matter.

She had had an inkling, kind-of/sort-of knew it all along. But still, the wave that hit when he finally said the words out loud, crossed that boundary—

I want you to matter.

The city brightened before her. Slowly and steadily. As if someone had their hand on the power grid and were raising the lever, higher and higher, on up through the red line. Multi-colored crowns caught fire, blurring together, and soon the skyline appeared as one single great blue and white flame and she wondered if it had ever looked prettier to her when her entire vision blurred at once.

How many times would she do this?

How many times—the insane persistence with which she drove herself to unhappiness, so convinced a positive outcome must surely lie ahead if she kept saying no.

Was it because she had loved twice and that made her afraid? That maybe love wasn't real or like she once dreamed. If three times, then why not four, five. Each meaning something less. Or nothing at all. How the lows lasted so much longer than the highs. And hurting someone else—God, it's so much easier to be hurt than to hurt someone else.

But she needed it. More than anything she wished she did not, wished she could go about this life string-free. But she did. She needed companionship. A partner. A friend. She needed it.

And so why not him?

Why not the boy laying like a tourist beside her.

Why not the accountant?

The one who went to church every Sunday. She did not, but she appreciated that he did. Someone who could believe in something greater than himself, this city beneath him.

She faced him. His hands were folded beneath his chin. Two minutes had passed since his declaration. She envisioned his total loss of hope in her. Hoped she could do right by him with the truth.

"This whole night," she said, "do you know what I've been thinking about?"

"How you can swap apartments?" he deadpanned and she cringed at her lack of subtlety. Composed herself again.

"I've been thinking of ways to break up with you."

"Less funny," he said, pushing himself upright in his seat. "Did you come up with one?"

"That's the problem. I don't think I want to."

She anticipated a second joke which never came. He and his five hundred sun freckles would wait for her.

Angie shied away and drew a sip of her beer. Tasted the warmth of her hands. Found courage in a half-torn label.

"So I was thinking about how I could end this—or, since I don't know if you could call what we've been doing even dating—ending it anyway. Then I thought of reasons why I shouldn't. And to be honest, I'm still confused. Except I feel like I want to try. But I don't think that's fair either. To drag someone around, just to try. At least not without being up front about it. And so what would you say if I told you I wanted to try, because you seem really decent, but inside I'm afraid I'm going to hurt you?"

She returned to him, expecting revulsion, instead she saw peace. A gentle smile which absorbed her words like he had absorbed the city all evening. She began to believe he might be the type who could absorb anything at all.

"Do you know what the best part of dating at our age is?" he said with a pause. "Experience. You feel like you've seen it all before.

"Do you know what the worst part is?" he continued, waiting this time for her response.

"What?"

"Experience. You start to wish you could do it all with a fresh heart again."

She was meant to laugh but could not answer, could only shrink in her own shame, the lameness of her proposal.

"I think what you're asking for, Angie, is permission. To hurt me one day if you need to. And if that's the case, then you have it. Go ahead, hurt me. I'll sign anywhere for that chance.

"But something tells me that won't make you happy either. You'll feel like I just kicked the burden back to you. Which is true, until you realize the permission you're really asking for isn't mine to give."

He lowered his bottle to the ground between them. When he looked up again, every light in Manhattan seemed to reflect in his eyes.

"Of course my answer is yes, Angie. But if you really mean to try," he reached out his hand, "I want you to be a yes, too."

Two billion lights—

She had been asked that once in an interview: 'How many lightbulbs are there in New York City?'

At the time, she guessed a billion.

Afterwards, she googled the answer of two.

But now, with half the night past, and New York City dimmed, maybe her original guess was closer to right.

One billion lights shining.

As she rose, the nerves in her legs firing after nearly three hours at rest, she hoped that, when she leaned over him, and he gazed up to find her, his hand still arched towards her empty seat, there was a way for her to block out every one.

7

IT'S CHARLES.

Inside, with his back turned. Sandy hair cropped and dulled with salt. His head bowed down and still.

He's sitting so still.

She wants to smother him with hugs. Shake him back to life.

She wants to run away. Protect him from her.

She has done it before, could do it again—walk away, become a ghost. It had been for the best.

But seeing him now, frozen in his booth like a diorama in a museum, plus her own feelings—had she missed him this much?—she questions, who was better for it?

She opens the door. The bell chimes. His gaze remains fixed on his tea even as she steps beside him.

"Hello, Charles."

He tilts upwards. Blinks twice. Recognition blinding.

This is the moon passing, she thinks.

This is the end of the eclipse.

All those memories you've stored. You can put them away now. I'm here.

His face pinches and she thinks tears might form, until—

"Hello, Snowflake," and now it is her face pinching.

That name—

Snowflake.

So many others guessed, tried to borrow its meaning for their own, a puzzle to solve. Except Charles. Charles had it wrapped so early, had been so consistent from the start. He got the one free pass. Never a puzzle at all, but her. Fundamentally and vitally *her*.

He notices the bulging Strand bag at her side.

"It's not Shakespeare," he says.

"And Shakespeare isn't you," she answers, sliding into the booth and resting her hands on the table near the edge where she does not think he will reach.

Unless he does, she thinks.

He deserves that chance.

From three feet, he studies her. She studies him.

The boy is gone. He will always appear young, but no bouncer will challenge him again. Creases, the product of a perpetual tan. A half-inch scar, new to her, fades into his cheek like a dimple. Even his clothes—a collared shirt for the occasion—suggest a man, if not taught, then seeking to act his age.

"Still black, two sugars?" he asks.

"Yes, please."

"I wasn't sure what diet you'd be on, but the peach cobbler was calling me. You can have some if you want," he says, inching his plate forward. "Or something else."

"Coffee is fine, thanks."

"So be it," he answers, raising his hand into the air. Angie braces for a patented "*Mademoiselle!*" which never comes. Did he finally upset a waitress after riding years of impossible charm?

"A coffee, please," he requests as the waitress, a short woman with orange hair, passes.

"So what important business brings you back to the great big city?" Charles asks.

"Nothing exciting," she answers. "Meetings."

"Not exciting to you, perhaps. But, I assure, it is to others. You know there is an assumption New Yorkers stop caring once their transient children leave. You, however. I've had many people ask about you. The wondrous places you will go."

"Like Delaware."

"Yes, the Diamond State. Much like you. A diamond."

"Still full of flattery."

"A gift and a curse."

"Mostly a gift."

"Then it is. If you say so."

"Have you found anyone?" she asks, too quickly.

"Would you be here if I had?"

"Yes."

"No. No woman will keep me, and I have found too few worthy after the likes of you. And others. I'll say others so as not to press you in to guilt. But, yes, if you'll allow me to boost your ego, you stand high on the mantle of all-time greats."

"I'm not that good."

"If only it was for you to decide."

Blood courses through Angie's cheeks.

The orange haired waitress returns, lowering Angie's coffee. Charles places her two sugars beside the saucer.

He waits patiently as she pours then stirs the sugar into the black, the spoon clanking against the mug. Stays silent longer as she takes a first sip she wishes had preceded any drinking this evening, life and reason returning to her at once.

"Do you mind if I get right to it?" she asks. "It's been a long night."

"They're all long nights. And no, I would expect nothing less."

"What is it, Charles? What are you trying to say? Is it me? Is it us? I know I owe you a long overdue apology, but I thought we were past this. But if we're here now, we must not be. That's what I've been trying to figure out all night long, chasing around the city, all my haunts. If there's something to say, why not just say it?"

"It's not just meetings, is it?"

"Is this another clue? I'm sorry, Charles, I don't think I can take any more clues."

"I lost the only clue I had a long time ago, Angie. Now it's you losing me."

"So you have no idea, about tonight?"

"I know I am sitting across from Angie Seaglass, excuse me, Angie Hart, at our diner, four years, seven months after I last saw her. That's it."

"How did you know I was here?"

"You don't do conversations except in person. You never have. If I receive a text, I know you're in town."

"Then what did you want?"

"You mean now or when?"

Angie sighs inadvertently. It is possible, she thinks, the whole world is as lost as she is.

"Let's go with now."

"Well," he says, cutting into his peach cobbler, lifting a piece, contemplating. "Are you sure you don't want some?" he asks.

"I'm sure."

He nods and bites. Closes his eyes to savor. Lowers his fork onto his napkin.

"You know I had this big speech planned years ago. When I thought it mattered a whole lot. I don't know what it says that I hope it still does. Not very good at moving on, I guess."

"What is it?"

"My own long overdue."

Angie feels her guard rise. Ancient anxiety screaming back. She prepares a swift, "No." Hangs it upon the same wall she built years ago.

"To apologize," he says.

Her wall crumbles. Into a billion little pieces.

"For what?"

"For being me. For not letting you go."

"But you did. Eventually," she answers, forgiving what need not be forgiven.

"No I didn't. I was selfish. I'd walk past Dymphna's or somewhere, see you with Geoff, and text you anyway. Wait for you to not text back.

"I saw you happy and I couldn't accept your happiness didn't include me. I treated you poorly for a long time and put you in more than a few compromising positions," he shifts his fork in line with his knife. "I told you a lot of selfish things, but I never told you that when I saw you, I saw you happy. Happier than I've ever seen you. Or, that I knew more happiness lay ahead for you."

She fights an urge to steal his hand from across the table, cup it as he boulders through.

"If you love somebody," he continues, "and I do love you, Angie, saying that the right way for once, you help illuminate their happiness. With Geoffrey, I saw you happy. If I really love you, I need to tell you that.

"That's my apology. What I'd been hoping to say, what I tried to say towards the very end. I love you, Angie. I'll always love you. The right way."

Now she does take his hand, grasping as tight as she can, wishing there was some piece of Charles she could take with her and keep forever.

He presses back apologetically. Feigns a smile to cheer her.

"But that's not why you're here, is it?" he says, returning her hand to her side of the table.

"It wasn't you," she answers.

"I wish it was."

"No, tonight. The reason I'm here. I thought it was you. Part of me was hoping it might be. But—"

"But what?"

"But...I have to go," she says and his face melts, revealing the four years and seven months he spent waiting.

As she grasps her coat, she reaches for him with her open hand.

"We're going to stay in touch, Charles. We're going to catch up on everything. Because I want to hear everything. Every last detail of your gorgeous life. And I want that to be my apology. That I haven't said goodbye. That I'm not saying goodbye to you now. I won't do that again. But I do have to go."

"Go, go," he waves. "Do what you need to do. Find the important people!" he laughs, his encouragement raising Angie's spirits more than a thousand coffees ever could.

She pauses above him.

"I do love you, Charles. You know that, right?"

"I do," he answers and she prays he believes it.

"Can we share that peach cobbler next time?"

"Any dessert you choose."

"Goodbye, Charles," she says. "But only for a little."

He winks.

"Goodbye, Snowflake."

8

A SLIVER OF LIGHT CUT across the bed, slicing her stomach which she rubbed with her fingers, squeezing skin into thin rolls. With her hand she poked and patted as if that were a way to decide. Like flipping when there was no coin to flip. Just a belly to rub. A tummy to tap, tap, tap. Drumroll please.

Only a body.

Only skin.

What difference? Her hands or his?

The light expanded over her chest. She rolled her head only to catch a high shadow flinch as the door shut again. Back to darkness. A muffled, "Sorry," from behind.

Hot, she kicked the covers beneath her feet. She had nothing to hide. He had seen this all before.

Then again, so had she.

Their clumsiness was enough to cringe. The inevitability stemmed by his, "I'll be in town..." her, "It's been long enough," consent. "A drink—" of course, three, four, a stranded fifth. Add the sad convenience of his spouse and her boyfriend each a continent away. A hotel room—his—at The Standard.

Worse, her failure to foresee this, the decision point, taking place not on some restaurant's stoop—hand in hand, a brow raised with suggestion, falling with good sense—but with him pacing tiles as she drummed to light spots dancing along the invisible ceiling.

A thump sounded. An urge to ask if he was okay came and faded. Impatience destroying desire. Thoughts turning to others:

The name of his high school girlfriend was Pierce. She was a family friend from Boston, their romance bloomed by summers on The Cape. He once told Pierce he loved her, too, and even though they had broken up, she applied anyways to NYU.

How had Pierce reacted when she got the news? Had she wondered, stuck beneath the Washington Square Arch, who was this lucky girl down in Texas?

The lucky girl in Dubai was named Scarlett. She was British and if Angie held any resentment towards her it was only the banality of it—his desert romance with a polo-shirted brunette who spoke in Queen's English.

But no, no animosity. What use when love is so clearly a matter of place and time. Scarlett's great sin was finding herself in the right place at the right time, falling for a boy who, more than anyone, compartmentalized his loves into very specific places and very specific times.

And so Angie—being *his* memory of Texas, *his* memory of New York—drummed and wondered if that made this okay. Together, in *their* place. Come-to-grips that One True Love might not exist, but instead some other transcendence lingering. A long sensational pull. The urge now, the curiosity, the need to acknowledge that feeling. Angie and Teddy. Forever, it seemed, tied at the hip.

He ran the faucet. Next would be the shower. However many distractions a bathroom might afford. She could join him, surprise him in the steam's mist. Leave him no choice. Or she could slip away. Leave behind a clean conscious, an open bed, and a trail of what ifs.

Instead, she turned over and succumbed to the effects of all that drinking. Felt the cool bed absorb her. So much worth trusting in a good night's rest, she thought. The simplest decision of all.

She sighed in tribute to this latest of life's twists. Imagined what might happen if she were to fall asleep—would he simply lie down beside her, same as old? She fixed the pillow. She shifted her legs. She made a wish.

Why shouldn't there be a wish?

But not for her. Certainly not for him. They had done enough to bungle the lives of others, try not to imagine the wake of hearts spared if they could have made it work the first time.

For Charles—the deserving one. A wish he would not be crushed by this, a given. That he would finally see she was tired, could no longer keep up, she hoped. The truest wish: for his own happiness. That he could find a Scarlett for himself. Someone with a sense of adventure to match his own.

Charles deserved adventure. He deserved happiness—

Light flooded the room.

Too soon, she thought.

She spun her head. In the door frame he stood, a silhouette in boxers. Chicken legs and pointy joints.

"Something's—" Teddy mumbled.

"What?" Angie asked, rolling over in plain view.

"Something's wrong," he repeated.

"Say it," Angie pressed.

He drew a breath. Knocked on the frame for courage.

"I'm married..."

Angie glanced at the covers kicked down to the end of the bed. If they had been closer or she more awake, she might have ripped them over her head, then screamed and howled until hoarse, cursing every living fate which had brought the two of them together and more.

But the sheets were too far away. She too unsurprised. All she could muster was to sit up, draw her legs in, naked, but what did that matter, and rest her chin on her arms, moving occasionally only to brush her soaked eyes against her forearms.

In silence, Teddy began to motion about the room, gathering his things—pants, shirts, a lost tie found behind the guest chair—while she tracked him from the bed.

Twice he paused to face her. Each time he winced like a wounded animal when he saw her puddled gaze stuck to him unblinking.

Chill swept her skin. Followed by goosebumps. Still she did not move. Did not reach for a pillow or a blanket. Only stared. Wanting to see if this was actually how he would leave her. Left behind in his own hotel room. Discarded for a second time.

At last, Teddy stood at the corner by the door. Suit on, tie dangling, a frightening impression of Josh Baskin going home.

"We're never going to see each other again," she said. To him, to herself, to the memories of when if someone spoke either of their names it meant both.

Teddy nearly collapsed. It was as if a string holding him from the ceiling had been severed. He found support on the chest in front of the T.V.

"That's what this is, isn't it?" she sniffed. "Not what we were trying to do, but—" she considered. "This is what needed to happen."

Tears dripped down his cheeks. Actual tears. The first she had ever seen from him. He caught them in his mouth and she saw his tongue swipe his upper lip with the forgotten taste.

"Is there anything you want to say?" she asked.

"I—," he tried.

"You what?"

"I don't know if I'm allowed to say..."

"You can say whatever you want Teddy. It's your life."

"But without it, you know."

"Without it meaning more to me than to your wife?"

He must have seen her shiver because rather than ducking in shame he stepped forward, lifted the comforter and draped it around her twice. He even tucked the fold in tight beneath her chin before returning to the chest.

"You're—" he fought once, rocking forward. "You're the happiest I've ever been, Angie. You made me the happiest I've ever been."

She could not free her arm from her cotton cocoon so she dabbed her face on the comforter instead.

"And I hope there are bigger things ahead," he continued, "I believe there will be. For both of us. But if this was the starting point. If we were one another's starting points. And you're asking me how I feel, how I think of you, or what you mean to me," he sucked in and exhaled, all tears and mucous, "I see you and I see the person who made me happier than everything so far. I see you and...I'm in awe. Of life. You're my best example of how perfect it can be."

Anger. Confusion. Sympathy. Pity. Love. Loss. Want. Hate. *Years* of hate and shame. Disappointment. Pride. Rejection. Acceptance. And God, how or why this—joy. Every emotion she had ever felt, it seemed, the tall broken branch six feet in front of her.

"I'm stuck," she said at last.

"You're not sure about something?"

"No, I literally can't move."

"Do you want me to loosen?"

"No, no," she answered. "Just come here and hug me."

He did. Enfolding her mound as she buried herself within him and it. Hoping he would squeeze her and squeeze her and squeeze her and squeeze her until there was nothing left for him to squeeze.

"You were the one," she said. "You were the one."

9

"RIGHT THIS WAY, Mrs. Hart."

"Thank you," Angie replies, stunned by her own police escort holding the gate.

"You'll find my partner up top. Take as long as you need."

Angie nods—*two* escorts—as she passes through the gate and climbs. On every fifth step, of course, a vinyl snowflake.

"There she is!" shouts the second, younger officer standing atop the concrete staircase with his chest puffed out. "The lady of the hour!"

"Have you been waiting long?" she asks.

"Not long, Mrs. Hart. If I had to guess, you're keeping right to schedule."

"So there's a schedule," she says aloud, object of the night's parade.

"There's always a schedule," he laughs. "Mine says I got about seven hours left."

"Not on my behalf, I hope?"

"Only if you plan on spending seven hours up here."

"I'll try to be quick then," she says, gazing ahead.

"Pretty simple, just follow the snowflakes. You have the park to yourself. I'll be behind as precaution."

Precaution, she smiles. The earnestness of his duty.

She reaches out her hand, "Thank you, Officer."

"My pleasure," he replies with a reddening face.

The destination she knows—where the snowflakes will turn right and the great white frame will appear. With stadium seating, her treehouse in the city. Above the street yet beneath the sky. In between. Hidden and not quite, still a part. Vulnerable to the writers and romantics, that teenage magician who once promised, then failed, to make every car on 26th Street vanish.

Arriving, an added touch reveals: a silk handkerchief laid for her, ice blue with a snowflake sewn in the middle.

Every detail, it seems.

She sits before the frame like a viewfinder, allows the film to play: a glossy intersection, a green light. On the edge of the frame, pedestrians like perfect extras march against the cold, bundled up while looking down. *Action!* Two vehicles streak from underneath, racing to catch the next light.

The scene she finds comforting in a way she cannot easily describe. Only that it feels like escape, separating from the city's flow. Levitating, nearly; out of body, if the street is where a body belongs. Reflection, she finds, so much easier twenty feet above.

Recall conversations with friends. The capital B, capital N, Big News shared on these benches, coffees or Thermosed wine in hand: Kristin's pregnancy, Nell's engagement then divorce, Audrey's dream-chasing decision to break for Spain. Delaware. Nell had been here and buoyed her through that.

Geoffrey, she considers, in brief visits. His wordless acceptance of the High Line as her sanctuary while he chose Hudson River Park for his own. That jog offering Angie's only legitimate jealousy yet—Geoffrey's obsession with water. As if Lake St. Clair had been a gateway. Here the Hudson and maybe one day follow it and find him wide-eyed in the center of the Atlantic.

And, suddenly, it clicks.

This night. Its purpose.

So embarrassingly simple.

So naggingly sweet.

Leave it to Angie to confuse her own favorite places.

Dymphna's, for example. Forever assigned as belonging to that period Before Geoffrey. A case of first memories high jacking the rest. Nostalgia sledding behind discovery. Why hadn't she encouraged them to find a new place sooner?

Count Strand, as well. The magical place she never belonged. An accident she ever sought it, even more inappropriate she went on chasing that tingling what-if feeling each time she entered. Not looking, her search by state and God declared over, but even after, did she find a bookstore more romantic than any barstool? Yes. Not fair to him that for a long while, the answer was still yes.

Where next? she worries, discouraged by her misjudgment, frightened by her misgivings.

How well could he possibly know her? How would he ever guess? That behind each door he opens she finds confusion. Within every haunt, a ghost haunting.

It is her fault. She tangled the web. Slowly, over years. One date at a time. She allowed them to fall in love in places she had fallen in love before. And here he is, stepping brilliantly but blindly through this history of hers she never shared.

She cannot let him go on. Cannot let him stumble. There are nerves ahead, waiting to be exposed. And what if he were to miss completely? Choose a place like Times Square where she once had them take their Christmas photo in jest—

Yes, he knows her better, but the chance to slip is real. He has never faltered once, why help him now. Not when it would be her own faults, her own indiscretions, her past, this impossible city, obstructing his beautiful intentions.

"Where are you?" she asks out loud, wanting him beside her. His body, his voice. Wanting to speak to him before she can cause any more harm alone.

She pulls her phone from her coat.

"Be there, be there," she prays to the sound of the first ring. "Be there—"

Music.

She hears music.

Muffled, but near her, playing.

She circles her head, removes the still ringing phone from her ear.

It is their song. Colby Wilson's voice.

There are no speakers behind her. Before her, the benches are bare. The sound is closer than that.

Below her.

The sound is beneath her.

She reaches under the bench, feels the shape of a box, and pulls, tape tearing free.

Ice blue with a white ribbon.

She unthreads the ribbon. As she lifts the top from the box, Colby Wilson's voice erupts—*Saving all our penny cents...*

Inside is Geoffrey's phone. Her name, *"Angie MoMA,"* lit bright on the screen.

We danced all night...

She ends the call.

The music stops.

Silence returns to The High Line.

She stares at his phone in disbelief. Her own beside it. Roiling within her stomach: the sense of disconnect when she is without her phone, magnified ten times by having his.

He stranded himself.

Stranded them both.

Trusting she would find him.

But where? she panics as the street blurs before her and the cold for the first time pierces her senses.

At the top of the landing the young officer stands with his back turned. She feels foolish asking him, a boy no more than twenty-five, for help.

What would she even ask?

She faces forward, collects the ribbon along with the top of the box which had fallen. Determines she will put them back together, nice and neat, gift him his phone back in the box when she finds him. When he finds her.

The box bottom lies on the bench. She reaches for it and discovers an envelope hidden inside. Ice blue with a white wax seal. A snowflake pressed into its center.

She tears the envelope, removes a letter.

Dear Angie,

First, an apology. A friend should not wait five years to meet their friend's significant other. I could give you excuses—two children and a business which seems less like the rocket ship it's portrayed as and more like a third disobedient child—but they would be merely that, excuses. I have known of your role in Geoffrey's life from nearly the start. And from that start, I have never known Geoffrey to be so full of joy. Please believe me when I say it will be one of the great pleasures of my life meeting the woman who has brought such joy to my friend.

Second, I must admit, perhaps as you do now, I thought this a rather silly concept when I first heard it. I asked him: "You're going to send her on a wild goose chase through Manhattan in the dead of winter?" Geoffrey then reminded me of a previous time I had called him silly. A beautiful woman had exited a bar in Gramercy on a night like this. "Oh well," I said, pleased our stars had aligned for a few brief minutes of conversation. Less satisfied was my friend. "Keep going," he said to me. I have since met Prime Ministers and CEO's of the world's largest corporations, none made me so nervous as the trip out that door. And no advice so important. I now call that beautiful woman my wife.

Keep going, Angie. Our loving friend might be a silly one, but that is also why we trust him with all our heart.

Your loving friend,
A.J.

Angie lowers the letter. Through the white frame, on the street beneath, a snowflake lights the rear windshield of a town car.

10

FIRST THERE WAS her grandfather, shouting from the foyer, "I have a date with my granddaughter!" When she appeared, only eight minutes late, in her violet velour dress, Adidas sneakers, and an Aero cardigan, he smiled, "I'll be the envy of every man in New York."

There were her mother's trailing worries—*don't let him walk too much, don't let him spend too much, don't stay too long*—entering his maroon Oldsmobile. As soon as the doors shut, he winked, "Are you ready for an adventure?"

There was the train station in Hartford. "Skip the line!" he declared, raising pre-purchased tickets. "We shall be like seasoned commuters," direct to the newsstand. "*The Wall Street Journal* for me and which periodical for you—*Time*, *The New Yorker*, or—what did you find there? *Cosmopolitan*? Impeccable."

There were his tales of New York as they breezed along Connecticut's shoreline. Eight years of shining shoes, bussing tables, and the courier job he secured at a patent office to pay for his subway tokens. "Paid for a whole career, turns out." In between, scenes of jazz on 52nd Street, movies at Radio City Music Hall, and baseball games at Ebbets Field.

There was the long, dark tunnel leading towards Grand Central. Him pointing up. "It's above us now," he said. "The greatest city in the world. And we're headed straight for the heart."

There was Grand Central itself. In a word: arrived. Riders pouring across the tan marble floor from dozens of gates. Beneath that starry ceiling, a surging belief she had made it to a place she was destined to be. Whatever New York held in store, this was the gateway. This was the entrance to a dream.

There was Lexington Avenue. The sidewalk a platform for what must be the most privileged people on earth. Locals striding with such purpose it was as if they were each stomping something impossibly large down to fit their needs. Up above, all around, the buildings, forever and ever to the sky.

There was the greatest building of all. From the top she could see Central Park, cut out like a center piece of cake. He taught her the five boroughs: Queens where he once wooed a Woolworth's girl, Brooklyn with its famous bridge, Staten Island a haze to the south, his first two years boarding in the Bronx, "And this," he said. "All this glory-to-man we're surrounded by, is Manhattan."

There was Times Square. The practical center of the universe. Surrounded by the biggest brands in the world: Coca-Cola, MTV, CK, Virgin, Kodak. Her skin tingling. A feeling that she stood at the vortex of everything that existed, and in that moment, everything that existed was focused on her.

There was lunch at Planet Hollywood along with their "Grown-up talk." She nodded her head while he explained that love is rarely a perfect balance between two people, that sometimes it shifts, and how that can be a good thing because it gives us special opportunities to show how much we really care—which she didn't believe, because love is love, but she kept on nodding until he said, "Okay, no more grown-up talk."

There was the play, but really, there was Belle. The actress, that is. Two acts mesmerized by, wanting to know about, wanting to be this actual, real life princess with a voice like a cartoon bird and hips that must glide through the city. When she left the theater, where did she go? Was she in jeans? What was her apartment like? What shows did she watch? Did she have a date every night? Was she in love?

There was her grandfather's reaction when the lights came up. "Magical," he sighed. "Just magical." She told him she loved it, too, but inside she prayed for a truer magic. One which would transport her to this place now. Skip these rotten teenage years. Let her be here. Let her be this beautiful. Let her be Belle.

"Can we go to Tiffany's?" she asked with increased urgency afterwards, certain that Belle-the-actress must shop there, and also, because Cindy Stahl had spent the school year flaunting a birthday bracelet. "Only to look?" And thus there was Tiffany & Co. with its steel doors and shimmering heaven inside.

There were silver necklaces, silver earrings, and silver spoons. Diamonds, emeralds, and rubies set as jewelry, set within figurines. There was her grandfather, with his own silver tuft of hair, leaning against the display case nearest to the door, in awe of his beautiful granddaughter in this beautiful store. As if it were right two beautiful things should meet.

There was the heart. A diamond necklace with a price tag costlier than love itself, but so stunning it would make Cindy Stahl dread every day of 9th grade.

She called her grandfather and asked, "Do you think they'll let me try it on?" loud enough the saleswoman would hear. The saleswoman, too smart by a mile, heard the shake in her grandfather's response and answered with a question, "Is this your first Tiffany?"

There was the excruciating walk across the floor. The case of sterling silver pendants like training wheels. "See the cross?" the saleswoman asked. "My father bought me one just like it. I still wear it." Angie rolled her eyes and scanned the pickings. A heart the same as Cindy Stahl's. A key she thought pretty but would never wear. A star. A ring. A snowflake.

There was the way it separated itself. Displayed beside the others and not. Understated. Unique. A snowflake in June. Stranger to admit, but true: how it felt like it was already hers. Had been hers. Would be hers. Always. Her snowflake. "This one," she pointed. "I like this one." Her grandfather nodded, "I do, too."

There was the incomparable high leaving Tiffany's. Her chest rising with an acute sense all eyes were on her. Mouths she would have caught absolutely agog if she had not kept her own gaze forward, believing in her new wings. That, like every girl in Tiffany, she now belonged on this sidewalk.

Of course there was the need for a literal cherry on top. A chance to spend one more hour as a New Yorker. "Can we get Frozen Hot Chocolates at Serendipity?" she asked, the same as Lindsay Gavin raved about. "Frozen hot chocolate?" he answered, charmed and perplexed. "That's something I'd like to see!" and picked up his pace.

There was Park Avenue with its parallel lanes and the light turned green. "Let's see if we can't make it," he grinned, showing off a sweets inspired strut.

There were her eight exact skips towards the median, feeling her necklace jangle on her neck and admiring the yellow tulips when she reached. Turning around.

There was her grandfather. Caught in the middle of the avenue. Left leg held straight like a board, right leg hopping for balance. His arm reaching skyward, grasping air.

There was her sprint back. Finding temporary balance when she caught him but not half enough strength to hold him.

There were her screams for help and the lights changing. Her grandfather assuring, "It's okay, it's okay," until he overspun and they suddenly faced a starting line of vehicles.

There was the van which honked as it veered around her head, bent two feet off the ground. The shocking surge in strength that came to her as more cars passed and she experienced, for the first time ever, blood rage.

There was her grandfather, so calmly, "Maybe if we just—" until once more they nearly toppled over when a voice arrived, "I got you, I got you."

There was the man in the navy suit taking Angie's place. The woman in beige heels, single handedly halting traffic. Together they cleared onto the sidewalk where her grandfather collapsed on a planter bench and the man in the navy suit pulled a portable phone from his briefcase and called for help.

There was her first ride in an ambulance, in the front seat. Next, her first visit to an emergency room. Side by side with her grandfather, then alone for three hours. A brief panic when the new shift could not find him. Discovering him on the 17th Floor.

There was him telling her he was sorry from the hospital bed, rubbing his bandaged and braced knee. "I went and ruined our special day." "No you didn't," she promised him.

There was her mother's arrival. A train of hysterics. *I told you—, I have work in—, You can't—, I can't—, We'll talk in the—.* Then in and out and in and out of the room until the doctor was finished and the paperwork completed and they were asked to leave for the night. As she kissed her grandfather goodbye, he whispered, "Be nice to her," and winked.

There was the ride back to Mansfield. None of the promised talk. No talking at all. Two-and-a-half hours of silence as her mother drove with her hand cupped to her forehead. Not until they were home, and halfway up the dark staircase, did her mother clutch the bannister and address Angie. By what must have caught the only light, she settled on, "That's a nice necklace."

And there was lying in bed, inexplicably wide eyed, rewinding the day. The train ride. The Empire State Building. Times Square. The play. Tiffany's. The hospital—where one scene, one phrase in particular replayed itself. Again and again. Separating from the others. Stored, she knew, somehow, already, in that place where the most important memories are kept. The ones never forgotten.

Of her grandfather, whispering her close while her mother's voice shelled the hallway.

"That necklace," he said. "It looks so pretty on you."

Even in bed, she twirled the pendant in her fingers like she had then, like she always would.

"Do you know why I got it for you?"

"Why?"

"Because one day, a real nice boy's going to come around. And when he does, I want him to know who loved you first."

11

"ANYTHING STRIKING YOU, Mrs. Hart?"

"All of it," she answers as they pass what was once Rodeo Bar, a reclaimed derivative in its place.

"But not how you need."

"No, not yet."

"That's okay. We'll find it."

"Yes we will," she encourages, though after fifty-five minutes of driving, in circles from the West Village to the East, downtown and back again, she thinks she understands that finding is not the point.

To pick one location, a single special place in the whole city, with the most meaning, would be impossible. What he wants her to see—at least she hopes, otherwise she is more lost than she knows—is the city itself.

Here in her favorite state.

Asleep.

Because isn't that still the best myth to break, she thinks—this city, it sleeps.

Like watching a loved one, late at night, with feather breaths and closed eyes. Right beside and yet so far away. At their most precious. Not distracted by themselves. They just are. Leaving you free to marvel at their wonder.

And the wonder here is everywhere.

Chinatown and Little Italy, like set pieces each, borders drawn by electric banners. SoHo with its boutiques. Window displays that could cross upon the shadowed cobblestones and you would believe.

The U.N., rising beside First Avenue. Time jades, but still, that monumental hope. Or the side entrances to Grand Central, catching those ceaselessly swinging doors at rest. A brief respite before the great engine breathes again.

Take her back to that first night with Teddy. When rather than sleep in separate bedrooms he guided her from his parents' apartment on the Upper West Side down to the Lower East Side to watch the sun rise over Brooklyn.

They were so young.

The street smarts she assumed were his birthright. The way she trusted him as they trekked over needles in Alphabet City. Laughed with him when they lost an hour in Prince Street station, unable to read the service advisory. More important was the way he slept on her lap as they gypsy cabbed home amongst the delivery trucks at dawn, her new city waking. Not stupid, romantic.

It went by so fast.

That dawn. An entire decade of dawns.

Measure it by the number of storefronts she recognizes. When she first arrived, the bars and restaurants seemed endless. But give it ten years and it becomes an easy game to play:

Angel's, hiding above Stuyvesant Street—one and done dates worth it just to see their reactions as she snuck them through the Japanese restaurant. The Smith, ever reliable, ever pointing out the secret knot in the wood. Bar None, exactly once, with Geoffrey, empty on a wet night like this after seeing *Gravity*.

On and on, over and over. What use for this millennial FOMO—lusting over someone else's adventure—when adventure is on every corner?

Charles taught her that.

He broke the spell. Her useless need to fit in. He knew the best scenes were the ones you created for yourself. Leave it to others to want to be a part.

Also—he would insist—be open when they do.

Never forget the house party in Bushwick. The night she went from thinking of Charles as crazy-but-possibly-endearing, to still crazy, but in firm possession of at least part of her heart.

Starting with the girl in the watermelon print shirt. She entered with a Strand tote over her shoulder—same as Angie's, same as half the city's—and their host, a custodian of cool, scoffed *"Tourist."* It was such an inane comment, so clearly baseless, yet Angie had felt a cut of shame anyway, like maybe she herself had missed a chapter in New York's mythical code book.

While Angie stuttered, Charles snapped, "We're all tourists!" grabbed her hand, and rushed her out of the apartment in his own Moses moment which saw two-thirds of the party trail him to the corner bar none the wiser.

If he hadn't moved so quickly, she would have kissed him then.

"I hate that," he said on the L-train afterwards, in his to-her-now-famous rant. "The arrogance. As if their postage stamp of New York is better than everyone else's. Eight million people live in this city. From a hundred different countries speaking dozens of different languages, each representing this very second of time. Forget about now, in New York 2009, or New York 1999, which he wasn't even here for, try New York *1899*, it's different every second of every day, so what kind of asshole do you have to be to think your New York is the only New York because you took a dump next to Julian Casablancas in some dank bar in Queens the night Michael Jackson died.

"This whole city's a miracle," his voice pitched. "Every night is a miracle. The people you meet. The adventures you can have. What's wrong with being a tourist? Make it your own. Explore. Wear a fanny pack—"

And then she did kiss him. For the first time. As best she could, pinning him to the sliding door before he became so excited he said he had to stop or risk upsetting the nonexistent parents on a two A.M. train.

That was fun.

That was Charles.

Her own miracle. Heart the size of Manhattan. Defender of every inhabitant.

But also, each of them—Teddy, Charles, Geoffrey.

All three, to her, miracles.

This night is so much about them, she realizes. Purposely or not. Impossible for Geoffrey to know. But also impossible to imagine herself without. How inescapably connected they each are. How much of herself is composed of the three of them.

Teddy.

She understands now how a huge place can become small. Forgive him that and remember he delivered on his promise. He brought her here. To this place. To *New York City*. He made her dream come true and, while she was his—she does believe this—there was nothing and no one more important to him.

Charles.

From another world. He saw the enormity and sought to make it bigger. At every stage, after every reveal, remember it was in her direction he looked. She was his audience when the whole city was his trick.

And Geoffrey. Sweet Geoffrey.

Call her Goldilocks, but for her, just right. The one who found comfort in a city that isn't always comfortable. Her kind of tourist, or at least the kind she would like to be, would hope to be—fully aware of how brief and special this visit is. Able to treasure it, the way it is. Forever treasuring her.

And maybe that is closest to what she feels now. What Geoffrey always had, what it takes. Overwhelming gratitude. To be loved once is such a gift. But three times. By three men who adored her. Three men who praised her. Three men unquestionably better than herself—

For years she worried love could be marginalized. If three loves, why not four, why not five. As if she had been around the bend, had already seen—another case of New York's moral superiority—that One True Love belongs to those who never leave home.

But if she is honest, then what else to call it other than a blessing. Shared with indebtedness. That these three men were important in her life. That they placed her in their lives at the very top. Some not insignificant bit of shame if she ever failed to do the same for them.

And, of course—answer to this ride, to this night—as the Flatiron Building slices Fifth and Broadway like the bow of a great big ship, there could be no other setting for such a privileged life than this city. For all her indecision, still her favorite place.

"Dmitri," she smiles, no longer impressed by herself, wanting to see, wanting to experience someone else's wonder. "Where would you go?"

"Where would I go?"

"If you were in my place."

"Oh wow," he hums, "that's a tough one. Let me see. Golden State was in town tonight. So it definitely would have been The Garden. But it's too late for that. On a normal night, I like jazz. So find a good jazz club—Smalls or something like that with my wife."

Music! she slaps the leather seat. How had she not thought of that sooner? The million shows she dragged Geoffrey to. Mercury Lounge. Rockwood. Bowery—

"But I'll be honest, Mrs. Hart, and I'm only saying this because you asked, at this hour, I think I'd like to go home. See my family. Because you know there's nothing better than going home at the end of a long night."

12

"TELL ME ABOUT DELAWARE."

So they were true. All the hyperboles.

Inspiring.

The perfect boss.

She believes in people, unimaginably. Shannon Pughe had actually said that—*unimaginably.*

Take the same question from near anyone else, picture a sallow detective over a dead body. Tag the typical, condescending lilt, Dela-*where?* Add pity, add shame. Write in: broken candidate, used goods.

Angie also liked—Laurel hadn't posed her biggest question mark as a question. She asked Angie to tell a story.

Tell me about Delaware, she had said, as if it were Prague at Christmastime, Kilimanjaro in spring. Babylon discovered, right off I-95.

Strange. To anyone who expected less, Angie would have delivered less, a lie. To Laurel, who appeared to treat this interview as a gift received rather than one so clearly given, Angie felt compelled to give more, truth.

"I needed a break," Angie spoke, wishing she were a proper storyteller for Laurel's sake, capable of turning Wilmington into Wonderland. "I needed to get away from the city. My husband was offered a position in Delaware, and I encouraged him to take it."

"How do you feel now? Did it work?"

"I think so. Though I wonder if my being here makes me a contradiction," Angie laughed.

"Not if it's what you want!" Laurel jumped. "I was thirty-one when I ditched D.C. to be with my grandmother in Iowa. Every day she told me I should be back east, chasing my dreams. When she passed, that's what I did, except now I'll always have that time I spent with her."

Saintly.

"I wish I could say Delaware's been equally rewarding," Angie responded.

"But you did what you wanted. And I'm sure your husband was grateful."

"He was." Still is, she thought.

"And now you're back!"

Yes, Angie nodded. Now she was back. One lie still standing.

"And, given that you're back," Laurel continued, "I want to know, what can I help you accomplish?"

Sleet began to stick to the window behind Laurel. Angie watched it multiply as her mind stuttered blank.

She had practiced form questions on the train. Listing her skills, her client list. Her strengths, her weaknesses. That one time she faced an especially difficult challenge. How she overcame it. Well tread exercises in looking backwards.

But looking forward. Attempting to picture a future which included this place. Her in it. She hadn't.

She couldn't.

Angie felt for Laurel who gazed at her like a blouse and blazered sun. So completely sincere. So fully energized by two women at a desk manifesting their own destinies. What burning sun wouldn't want another star shining back?

Only now, Angie realized, what she wanted was separate from anything Laurel could offer. Not as simple as this role, because God she would love it here if she felt it was where she belonged, but first the answer to that sad, dangling *if*—the hope, the need to find that place after searching so long.

"I want to drive myself again," she answered, strong as she could, trying not to disappoint Laurel.

"I love it!" Laurel lit. "The most rewarding part of my job is seeing others succeed, Angie. That's what I'm here to do. I want to empower you."

Angie straightened. Empower?

"I called your references," Laurel continued. "Jade, obviously, but Wes, Zoe, they each had amazing things to say about you. Your clients, as well. Nick Loft, in particular, raved."

Angie felt her world tilting.

"The Delaware thing, I know a lot of people would see it as a red flag. I personally love it. I re-hired Ellie Reynolds eighteen months after she went backpacking and we never thought we'd hear from her again. She came back a superstar."

Angie would stab Jade the next time she saw her. "It'll be good networking," Jade had said on the same phone call in which she cheerfully described her recommendation of Angie to Laurel Wood for the dream job Angie was woefully unqualified for even before she left New York for two entirely sideways years. *"Thanks Jade!"* Angie had answered, like a naïve twit.

"Clients. There is some overlap, but I can think of five or six others off the top of my head I would love your help on."

A scene of Geoffrey appeared in her mind: satisfied at his desk in Wilmington, unwrapped hoagie beside, none the wiser his wife's meetings in New York included an interview.

"And please don't let me scare you on the travel. It's not that bad. We try to bundle cities together."

This had been done to her before.

"Oh my god. I'm literally spinning. You're going to be such an asset in the room."

Was she about to do the same to him?

Laurel, who had been waving her hands in a tap dance of excitement, paused and leaned forward. "I should ask. Do you have any questions for me?"

A million.

One.

"Great, because honestly, I think I have only one last question for you, Angie."

What do I tell Geoffrey?

"When can you start?"

13

"JORGE, call the Missing Persons Unit! We found her!"

"Did you miss me, Fabian?"

"Miss you? Please. You just like all them other girls. They say they gone, but then I find them standing here at my door!"

"Just like *all* the other girls?"

"You know I'm messing with you. Come here and give me a hug, beautiful. It's good to see you."

"It's good to see you, too," she replies, squeezing Fabian who still smells of baby oil.

"You would not believe the stuff that's gone down since you left," he says.

"Like what?"

"Like how about right above you. Little Miss Work-out Pants got caught in the laundry room with a kid home from college. His parents tried to press charges but he was nineteen so nothing they could do.

"You remember the dentist in 18D, always sneaking in girls? His wife finally caught him. Tuggs in 7G married Lisa from 10B. That was cool. Your apartment, a family just left. Oh goodness, they were a pain in my ass. They thought I was their nanny. Mrs. Postlewaite passed I'm sorry to say."

Angie's heart sinks with the news. Mrs. Postlewaite often knocked with "extra" flowers she had bought from the bodega next door. Whenever Angie objected, Mrs. Postlewaite waved her off with her favorite lie, "I think the owner has a crush on me."

"And what about you?" Angie asks.

"What about me? Ohhh, that's right. You been gone longer than I thought. Wait 'til you see this. I got a new girl for you. Check her out."

"Oh yeah?" Angie laughs, missing her late night updates on Fabian's exploits. "Where'd you meet this one?"

"You'll see, you'll see," he grins, thumbing through photos. "Here."

He hands Angie his phone. A baby girl.

"Her name's Vanessa. Five months. Thank God she looks like her mother, but I like to rub it in she's got my eyes. Means her mother can't stay too mad at me either. I tell her it's like yelling at her daughter!"

"Congratulations," Angie smiles.

"Aw, thanks Angie. I never been more in love. You know all those girls we used to talk about? Driving me crazy? That was nothing. This girl's the craziest. And sometimes her mother, too. I got lucky, Angie. I got real lucky. How about you? Any kids?"

"No," she answers quickly. "Still me and Geoffrey."

"That's cool. That's cool. How is Geoff? Still carrying desks for old ladies?"

"Desks?"

"You didn't hear about that? One day he walked right past here with a big wooden desk hunched over his back and I said, 'Hey Geoff! You know you live here, right?' He could barely breathe. Huffed and puffed all the way to the top of the block. Felt bad 'cause I couldn't leave the door, you know."

"That sounds like him."

"Yeah it does. You wanna go up, by the way?"

"Up?"

"Your old place! No one's there," he says, disappearing into the doorman's closet. "They're renovating all this week."

"I really don't need to."

"Sure you do!"

"I do?" she asks, wisening to a trick.

"Of course. Memories and all that you-know-what."

"Fabian, was he here before?"

"Was who here?"

"Fabian..."

"I don't know what you're talking about."

"You don't?"

"You know me, Angie. I don't see nothing. I don't know nothing."

"All right," she concedes at last.

"Go on, beautiful. Have fun up there. Just be careful you don't step on any tools."

He hands Angie the key and she crosses the newly renovated lobby, redesigned for a sugar rush: confetti cake flooring and pop art featuring a large strawberry donut.

In the elevator, panels with rainbow sprinkles hang where once there were mirrors. Given her night, she considers, this might not be a bad thing.

Normalcy returns on the eighth floor. Bare industrial gray and white. She cedes to muscle memory. Fourteen-and-a-half steps. Third door on the right. Slight change—a bar handle in place of a knob.

Angie turns the key.

Paint cans and protective plastic sheets. A slab of uninstalled kitchen granite where the TV stand used to be. Opposite, the missing couch. Scratches on the floor where the dining table stood. Picture hooks left dangling, missing Geoffrey's trio of sailboats.

She skips the kitchen and enters the bedroom which, even in the dark, is a bath of light, so much brighter than she remembers. Hard to believe Geoffrey never challenged her choice of sheer curtains. She had liked the way the city poured over their bed.

Standing in the place she once slept, she imagines the mattress rising above her hip. To her right would be the night stand, and to her left, Geoffrey, forever the courteous sleeper, tucked in the shape of an S.

Lie down and sleep. The desire is there. On the hardwood if need be. So much so that she does, dirt and dust be damned, lie down, feeling the grooves of the parquet floor with her fingers, then against her head. Stare up—there it is, the same paint chip she always thought resembled California.

What a waste, she thinks.

Two city years. Gone like that. Seven hundred nights she can barely distinguish.

Drunk nights, sober nights, tired nights, restless nights. Mostly healthy nights, the fortunately few sick nights. Boring, unparticular nights. Home, dinner, TV, bed. Forgettable because she's already forgotten nights.

Did they go straight to sleep, did they at least have sex? If they did, was it making love or was it screwing.

Motioning because they should, or anyways a clock in their bodies seemed to reset.

So easy to become accustomed, she thinks. So easy to grow tired. Much harder to grasp she might one day miss it.

She eyes the door, the white frame around it, and wishes he would appear. Leaning against the jam, in a suit for his big reveal. Or better yet, just boxers and a tee. He could lie down here on the floor and wrap himself around her, skin warming, until they fell asleep. In the morning the workers could find them. "*Hello,*" she might laugh and they would understand, closing the door as she backed further into him.

Their room.

Him.

One gone to yesterdays, the other—

As if she needs reminding—on this night of all nights—she still has the best part.

He isn't gone yet.

And the sooner she finds him...

Angie bolts upright. Circles her head. All that sits within the bedroom is a tape measurer on the windowsill.

She backs towards the living room, lifting plastic sheets. Behind a work table she discovers boxes of new light fixtures. Blocked is the coat closet. The bathroom, though freshly redone—to her liking, actually, with black and white hex tiles—is void of snowflakes.

She turns for the kitchen.

Atop the final-days laminate counter sits a large box, ice blue with a white ribbon.

Not hiding at all, she thinks. Simply the single raised, clean service in the whole apartment.

She tugs the ribbon and the box unfolds itself.

At once, her night resets:

"What did you say you were doing?" she had asked.

"Flipping through our wedding album."

She rubs the silk cover for what must be only the third or fourth time ever. Where did he even find it?

"You said you picked a favorite?"

"The one of us dancing."

She pictures the photograph as she opens the album.

"I'm a silhouette, but you, along with your dress—"

Aren't there.

The page is blank. Empty. The photo removed from its frame.

She flips to the next page.

Empty again.

Same as the third, the fourth, the fifth.

Headings in place, but picture after picture removed.

She flips and flips and flips, panic rising with every stripped memory. Some buried beast of fear equivalent to the lack of faith she always held in herself, in the two of them together.

Had he set her up? Did he finally see it, see her, see them as nothing better than a failed attempt. Was he giving her what she for years had given him: total nothingness, made bare by this empty apartment, this empty album, this empty evening exposing the emptiness where a full person should be, should have been, loving him and fulfilling him like he had for her, as she lifts and dangles the album over the counter, hoping for one final forgotten photo to drop, when an envelope falls to the floor instead.

Long and thin.

With a red logo stamped on its corner.

tkts.

She drops to the floor alongside the envelope. Rips it open from the side. Pulls out a note.

I liked it here, too. We can come back if you'd like.

But first, grab your tkt – The show's about to start.

14

IT SEEMED a game. More entertaining than the place. Watch the boy trail behind. Watch him slip ahead. Lose him momentarily, find him again—behind a wall this time, too slow identifying a female anatomy. Raise eyebrows and see his freckled face assume the color of the painting. Slacken the line, move ahead. Pause before a canvas of what appears to be noodles dyed blue, reel him back in.

"I like it," he said, guessing she did, too.

In reality, not knowing if she liked it herself. How does one know? How to make sense of blue noodles or bricks piled on the floor. A shovel hung from the ceiling.

Move along, slacken the line again.

She wished she could record this somehow. That would be artistic. Very Charles-esque. Trace their movements with paint suspended in the air. Her spinning sun and his revolving moon wandering the museum, floor by floor. Streaks of yellow and gray thick enough visitors would have to duck beneath them.

Poor lonely star. Polite little fish.

Not until forty minutes into their visit, sitting before Monet's dazzling water lilies, did she remember she was supposed to be judging him.

Of him, in her judging attempt, she thought little. Which was not to say less, only surprised by her indifference. She worried she had become the dating equivalent of the weary traveler—former wanderlust replaced by glossy eyes and a suspicion the world's cities had all become the same, so why not stay home?

Still, she liked his name—the way he spelled it out fully on the app like the giraffe. And she admired his effort. Though she did not want to be seen carrying it, she was glad to have a white rose tucked inside her coat. Also, MoMA. While not a lightning bolt of originality, his choice had been an evolutionary step above the *grab-a-drink?* default of his peers.

So she had her game. And he, she guessed to his liking, had her for the afternoon.

At three P.M. their tickets instructed they proceed to the top floor for their turn at the current exhibition: *Today He Rises* by Petr Klein.

In the first room, Petr Klein himself, dressed in jeans and a white tee smeared brown, crouched over a pitcher's mound of clay. Atop the mound was the sculpted shape of a man, on his knees and elbows, reaching up. The next morning, they read, Petr Klein would destroy the piece and begin again.

They watched for nearly ten minutes as the artist three times fashioned and unfashioned the clay man's reaching arm, no pose to his exact liking. When they at last stepped away, the man had no arm at all.

The next room held black and white photos of the previously finished pieces. In some, the sculpted man stood nearly at a full stance. In others he appeared glued to the mound.

Angie read the analysis on the wall—"*Is the value in the creation or in the destruction? Here a master has created art he is willing to destroy. Yes, masterworks. Does that make him a masochist, perhaps a murderer, or is there beauty in letting go? It seems wrong that photographs are taken. The images themselves defeat destruction. Though who would also deny them? Lest these marvels exist only in our failing memories...*"—and wondered what she was missing.

"Which is your favorite?" Geoffrey asked.

At a loss, Angie responded, "Eight."

"How come?"

"It's my favorite number. Did you have a favorite?"

"The one he was building. 27."

"Is 27 your favorite number?"

"It's the one he made while we were here."

They worked their way down the museum, one floor at a time. He stood closer to her now which she attributed to tiredness seeping in more than any act of bravery. Of course, the seeping tiredness may have been her own.

On her mind was whether she should steam outfits for the week when he suggested they sit on a bench centered within a room of ten foot canvases each painted a separate single color.

Snap to, she told herself. Treat this like work. Give him five good minutes to find out if you like him or move on forever.

"I kind of like these," he said of the rudimentary paintings. "Not too complicated."

"Is that one even painted?" she asked, pointing towards a white canvas.

"If you look closely, there's a really stunning image of Mary. Only you can barely see it because it's white on white."

"Wait?" she stopped, squinting. "Really?"

"No," he laughed. "I'm pretty sure it's just white on white."

She shot him a challenging glance, though she was happy to hear him tell a joke after seeming so reserved. If he had been his own blank canvas, at least now he had a hint of color.

"Really, though, what do you think makes these so special?" she asked.

"I don't know," he considered. "Maybe it has something to do with being first. Seems easy to knock, but someone had to be brave enough to try. Like, imagine him in art school, everyone's painting still lifes, and over here he's like, *Bam!* I got it. White on white. You're either going to get an A-plus or an F. I give him credit for trying." He turned towards her expectantly. "What do you think?"

"I like your answer," she said, appreciating the thoughtfulness of his response, feeling suddenly pressured to match it.

She studied the colorful room. Blue, yellow, orange, green, and red. Like walking into a box of Crayolas. Funny, as well, the need for massive canvases. Almost like something a child might do if given the chance. Grab a whole bunch of paint and make it—

"I think I've got it," she said.

"You think you've got it?" he grinned.

"Yup. I figured it out."

"Okay, then."

"I think the key is, if you want to do it right, is first, like you said, you have to be the original one to do it."

"Got it. Be original."

"Exactly. And the second key is, and I feel like we've seen this all day, is if you want to make an impact," she held her finish for dramatic effect, watching his sea green eyes expand into oceans as he leaned closer, "you've got to make it really, really, *big*."

He laughed out loud. Two visitors clad in black turned with frowns. Maybe it was the colors on her mind, but that's what his laugh sounded like just then, as if he had splashed the Crayola box room and the two art trolls in their black leather jackets with his own spectrum of paint, splattering the silence.

"You know something?" he said, collecting himself.

"What's that?"

"I think you're right."

15

"HELLO, ANGIE!" he booms from atop the glowing red staircase. There is nowhere else to lead her. This is the end.

She climbs the ruby steps until she stands just beneath his bursting smile.

"Hello, A.J.," she says, reaching out her hand.

He lifts her to the top step and hugs her instead.

"This was far too long coming, Angie. One should make time for those that matter. I am sorry we did not meet sooner."

"I'm sorry, too," she says as he holds her by the shoulders and leans back.

"He told me you were beautiful, tried to send me pictures, but I said, 'No,' I want to see for myself. Even then I thought for sure I had the wrong room tonight. You are more than beautiful, Angie."

"Thank you," she replies, wondering herself how she had not recognized him sooner. Behind those clear frames—wholly supportive eyes. That smile—a direct link to his heart. And, remembering her manners, recalling the entirety of the night, she repeats, "Thank you, thank you, thank you."

"But you don't even know what it is you're thanking me for!" he laughs.

"For this. For everything," she answers and his face softens.

"This was him, Angie. He did this. I only did what a friend would do."

Including opening the High Line, she thinks, but knows he would never take credit, his contract of friendship so far above her own.

"Six minutes to spare," A.J. announces, checking his watch. "I believe you just won me a Corner Bistro burger."

"He didn't have faith in me?"

"Plenty in you, not half enough in me. You and that town car would have been on time if it meant shutting down 47th Street for a motorcade."

She considers he might be telling the truth when he chuckles, "If you really want something to thank me for: his original plan included Brooklyn! I told him one borough was enough." A.J. settles. "What did you think of all this, by the way?"

"I—" she thinks, and is quickly overwhelmed. The night only just occurred and in its place all she sees is Geoffrey. "I don't think I've ever done anything even close to this for him."

"In fairness," A.J. smiles, glancing about the square, "I don't think many have. But also remember," he returns to Angie, "it is in proportion to you. Somewhere, in ways you may not even realize, you give him reason to do so much. Try to think of this as your love shining back."

And it does, she thinks, shine. This scene about her, flashing and shimmering as she makes sense of herself standing atop the TKTS booth, of all places, amazed and ashamed and wondering why or what or how, that she could be the recipient of love so bright when the combined energy of her own love would fail to power any one of these screens, let alone a single bulb.

"There you go, Angie," A.J. comforts with his arms around her. "Before the show starts."

"The show?"

"Of course!" he grins. "Don't you realize where you are? What would Broadway be without a show?"

"It's not over?" she brushes her eyes.

"Almost, Angie. It is nearly over. No more clues. All that is left for you is to take a seat," he says, stepping down and revealing a last blue handkerchief beside where he had stood.

"I think, Angie," he says, reaching for her hands and cupping them with his own, "this has been as I wished: a very good night. I'll be wishing you and Geoffrey many more very good nights. Just like this," he tugs, his face an endless fire of hope and warmth. "Though, perhaps," he adds, tilting his head with a second tug, "you each might consider one or two movie nights in between."

Angie laughs, "Thank you," for a final time as A.J. uncups his hands and turns down the staircase.

He is halfway when he stops.

"I nearly forgot!" he shouts, climbing back towards Angie. "You'll be needing these." He reaches into his pocket and hands Angie a ring box. Ice blue with a white snowflake embossed.

"You'll know what to do," he grins, before exiting again, down the length of the staircase to the ground where he pauses for the view.

"Magnificent! Isn't it?" he shouts, spinning half-circles in wonder as he disappears left of the stairs.

Assuming her seat on the blue handkerchief, Angie absorbs the scene for herself. Spots of tourists pose for photos with their phones raised high. A jogger with reflectors bounces southwards past McDonald's. Two policemen stand watch in the center of the square—different, she sighs, than her two friends from the High Line.

She opens the ring box. Inside are a pair of ear buds. She removes the first when the lights go out.

All of them, at once. Every display, every billboard turned black, as if some great plug had been pulled. Only a row of streetlamps shine like floating stars.

Angie stands nervously. She searches behind the rail for A.J. who is gone from sight. In the center of the square, the two policemen stand casually, one with his neck arched towards the blank screens while his partner checks his watch.

A flash erupts—from the far end of the square. Beneath the New Year's ball a snowflake spins in giant revolutions.

Another flash.

The number *10* appears, centered and blinking in time with the revolving snowflake until...

9

A countdown. Angie inserts the first earbud.

8

7

Now the second. Silence.

6

5

"This is happening, this is happening," she murmurs, silly and stupid, but what else to say?

4

3

Here come the answers.

2

All of the answers.

1

Cut to black.

Total silence.

Angie removes one of the buds. It is quiet outside, as well. She looks about, her eyes still adjusting to the darkness, though her previous fears have subsided. She finds this peaceful now—Times Square tamed momentarily while the tourists twirl aimlessly about the dark like children with flashlights.

A piano chord rings through her ear. It sounds so pure. So close to home. Like if she blinked she might *be* at home, in his arms, slow dancing. She replaces the second bud and hums the words as a screen lights in gold above her left shoulder.

City days...

The video is shaky, but it is her. On the screen, thirty feet tall. At Dymphna's. Years ago. Hair past her shoulders. In tears laughing.

So far away...

A second screen flashes further down, above Express. Angie again. In Central Park. Eating ice cream.

We found a house...

A thin strip of video above *The Today Show*. Her, sideways in bed, the exposed brick of her Delancey Street apartment revealing the time and place.

Along the interstate...

A flash towards the end of the square. Biking across the Williamsburg Bridge. She remembers looking back, seeing him film her as she zig-zagged.

White picket fence...

Yankee Stadium rises above American Eagle. Whenever the Tigers are in town. To this day she doesn't care, but he does, and that makes it fun.

Made some sense...

Outdoor movies in Bryant Park.

Had a lot of fun...

Friendsgivings. Four of them in a row.

Saving all our penny cents...

In every direction now, screens flashing.

We danced all night...

A six-story sunrise in Montauk. A twenty-foot kiss goodbye.

Out on the porch...

Concerts at Terminal 5. Hammerstein Ballroom. Baby's All Right.

Whispered romances...

Restaurants—Hudson Clearwater. Balthazar. Tartine.

Through a screen door...

Bars—Jimmy's, just a few blocks away. Employees Only. The Other Room.

All our friends say...

MoMA.

We got it made...

Her photographs appear. His paintings.

I always had it made...

His sopping wet proposal—when they couldn't fly out—insisting she meet him on the roof during Hurricane Sandy.

With you, Babe...

The screens fade to black, before the chorus begins. Where is he? she wonders. In the pictures, in all these, only glimpses of him—a hand, the back of his head, but not his face, not his cheeks, not his sweet, nostalgic eyes. He had made her the world's biggest photo album, but where is he?

Fade in again. The end of the square.

A wedding cake.

But sometimes I want to go back...

Their wedding, displayed across two dozen screens.

I want to see what we made...

Before pictures, during pictures, the after party.

I want to see that it lasts...

Friends, family—her parents, together.

In the city that never fades...

Their first dance. What did he call it earlier tonight?

I want to see the lights in Times Square...

'The perfect white.'

I want to ride down Park like a millionaire...

And what had she whispered while they danced?

This life keeps getting better...

'This—'

I want to live forever...

Angie unlocks her eyes from the screens. Looks down. He is there. At the bottom of the stairs. He is there.

As long as forever's with you—

She rips both earbuds out, prepared to attack the steps two at a time, until he lifts his left hand up calmly as if to say "Stay," and for the first time she, who dangled this man, ignored, and even doubted for so long, feels at once dangled. She is his. Always. She will stay.

He reaches the step just beneath hers, where their eyes are level.

"It was you," she says.

"It was me."

"I'm sorry. I didn't think it was you and—I didn't know and—"

"It's okay."

"Then today—I never told you about, I didn't think she'd, I should have—"

"It's okay, it's okay. I knew."

"I'm sorry, Geoffrey. I'm so sorry."

"I love you, Angie."

"And you did all this anyway."

"It was for me as much as for you."

"I had forgotten so much."

"Me too, Angie. Me too."

"I won't ever forget again."

She clears her eyes to view his own sea greens. How had she ever seen anything less than a miracle in them? She slams her face into his, kissing him while their whole life together flashes in a hailstorm about them. Every memory ever captured and then—

She closes her eyes, pictures the screens spinning with memories still to be. Everything she will do for him. Their every after swirling about them like a dream.

"Forever," she breathes. "This. Forever."

IT IS 2:18 A.M. Times Square flashes silently. Here is the girl next door, six stories tall. Her face is a cosmos of freckles. In nine hours a boy from Oregon will gaze upon them and make a wish. Bright bursts: the trailer to a blockbuster, featured on a screen certain to dwarf any in which the full film will play. Turn to discover the phone of the future: thin as a human hair, faster than the human mind. The last evolutionary step before no physical trace remains. On 47th Street, a young couple exits a yellow cab, dressed for a dance. He holds her carefully about the waist, for her eyes are covered by an Oklahoma crimson scarf.

"Now?" she asks.

"Almost," he says, guiding her across Seventh Avenue where, underneath her heels, she feels the sidewalk rise.

"How about now?"

"Nearly there," he leads her to the exact spot he had chosen—at the north end of the square, facing south, in front of those glowing red steps.

She does not ask a third time. His hands, sliding from her waist, adjusting her shoulders just so, provide the answer.

One final pause.

This moment, for her, overwhelming.

For him, selfish. All that planning, not over weeks, but years. Envisioning, dreaming—

Finally, he is here.

And she is with him.

They made it—

To *New York City*.

They made it—

Together.

He loosens the scarf.

"*Now.*"

ABOUT THE AUTHOR

RICH WALLS GRADUATED from Villanova University in 2006. He is the author of *Standby, Chicago* and the creator of *One Page Love Story*. He lives in Hoboken, New Jersey.